Early Prevention Series

THE RABBIT WHO LOST HIS HOP
A Story About Self-Control

by Marcia Shoshana Nass
illustrated by Denise Gilgannon-Collins

Childswork™
ChildsPLAY
CALL 1·800·962·1141

A Brand of The Guidance Group
www.guidance-group.com

THE RABBIT WHO LOST HIS HOP
A Story About Self-Control

by Marcia Shoshana Nass
illustrated by Denise Gilgannon-Collins

Childswork/Childsplay publishes products for mental health professionals, teachers and parents who wish to help children with their developmental, social and emotional growth. For questions and comments, call 1-800-962-1141.

© 2004 Childswork/Childsplay
A Brand of The Guidance Group
www.guidance-group.com

ISBN 10: 1-58815-061-5
ISBN 13: 978-1-58815-061-5

Introduction

It is common for young children to have problems in self-control. While some may have a biological predisposition towards developing an attention deficit disorder, most have simply not learned the "skills" of self- control.

If you want young children to learn self-control, the first thing to do is to be a good role model. For better and for worse, we live in a culture geared to satisfying our needs quickly. We have become accustomed to overnight delivery of packages, high-speed Internet access, and an instant cash machine on every corner. And when we don't get what we want as quickly as we want it, we typically become impatient. Too often, we show our impatience in ways we would not want children to see. Books like *The Rabbit Who Lost His Hop* explain to children, and also remind adults, that self-control is a virtue in every aspect of our lives.

The second thing adults can do is to give children opportunities to practice patience and self-control. Children need time and encouragement to work puzzles, build block towers, and experiment with art media. Television entertains children, and sometimes even gives them important information, but it does not teach them self-control. Children need to learn to do activities that require their concentration. All children, and particularly children with impulsivity problems, should have their TV time limited and their time with video games and computers closely monitored. A healthy diet, adequate sleep, and exercise will help produce the brain chemistry associated with good self-control.

Finally, adults should teach impulsive children the thinking and behavioral habits that lead to self-control. Children can be taught to monitor their actions and thoughts, to be aware of their behavior and how it affects others, and to calm themselves down when they are too excited or overactive. This book can be the first step in teaching children these skills. Patient and caring adults will make the most important difference in helping young children with their emotional development. I prescribe 15 or 20 minutes every day to teach children self-control and other good behavior habits. It is always better to treat potential problems early. Remember the old adage, "An ounce of prevention is worth a pound of cure."

Lawrence E. Shapiro, Ph.D.
January 2004

ACTIVITY SHEET

The Childswork/Childsplay Early Prevention Series is designed to help young children learn about common emotional and behavioral problems and acquire skills that can help prevent these problems from becoming serious. *The Rabbit Who Lost His Hop* tells the story of an overactive young rabbit, Ricky, who is so impulsive that he can't control his hop. With the help of a counselor, he learns to stop, to relax through deep breathing, and to think about his choices.

This book can be used to help impulsive or overactive children understand that other children have similar problems and that there are things they can do to learn self-control.

The following are some activities you can do using the Ricky Rabbit doll to help reinforce the lessons of this book.

Role Play
The great thing about books that have a psychological message is that children like to hear them over and over again. Every time they hear the story, its message gets a little clearer. When children act out the story, the message becomes even more important to them.

The adult can narrate the story and take the role of the other characters, while the child uses the rabbit doll to act out the role of Ricky. If the child is a non-reader, the adult can simply tell the child what to say.

Make Up Plays with Ricky and Other Dolls
You can also encourage a child to make up plays, using the Ricky Rabbit doll along with other dolls. Perhaps Ricky can teach a super-villain action figure to be more thoughtful. The child can also use Ricky to act out scenes from his own experience.
You may want to make a videotape of the dolls acting out a story, which the child can then watch. A basic rule to remember is that the more a child sees a positive image of himself conquering a problem behavior, the more he will able to cope with the real situation.

Practice the Stop, Relax, and Think Technique
You can use the Ricky Rabbit doll to act out the stop, relax, and think technique described in the book. Have the child practice deep breathing, using the doll. Then, talking to the doll, ask the child about good choices and bad choices in his behavior.

Use the Ricky Rabbit Doll as a Reminder
Young children often attribute magical powers to their toys. A child may want to have the Ricky Rabbit doll as a reminder that he can control his impulsivity and behave in appropriate ways.

Note: Impulsivity and overactivity are character traits. Not all impulsive children have psychological problems, but some do. If you are a parent or teacher concerned about a child's impulsive or overactive behavior, consider having the child evaluated by a qualified expert. There are many techniques and strategies that can help these children make a better school adjustment and develop better behavioral and social skills.

Ricky Rabbit lived in a beautiful brick house in Rabbitstown with his mom and dad. Ricky had everything he wanted. He had the latest toys, the coolest games, and the most amazing comic book collection.

But there was one thing Ricky did not have—his hop. He had lost it when he was just a small bunny.

When he was younger, Ricky could hop. He would hop, hop, hop all around. His mom and dad said, "Ricky, you have the best hop in all of Rabbitstown." In the family photo album, there were pictures of his mom and dad measuring his hop and smiling proudly.

But as Ricky grew up, he began to race and run up and down and all around. While the other rabbits were still hopping happily along, Ricky was whizzing by.

"Why can't you just hop like you used to?" asked his mom.

"Why do you have to run, run, run all the time?" asked his dad.

But Ricky just could not slow down.

One Monday morning, when Ricky woke up, he heard the wind scattering leaves on the ground. Summer was ending, and autumn was on its way. It was the first day of the new school year at Rabbitstown Elementary School. Ricky was most unhappy because he did not like school.

I will just get in trouble again this year, thought Ricky. *I wish I could stay home and play with my computer games.*

"Ricky, brush your teeth and get ready for school. It's almost time to go," said his mom.

Yuck, thought Ricky. *Yuck, yuck, yuck.*

Mrs. Carrotson was Ricky's teacher this year. Ricky liked her smile, and she seemed really nice. *Maybe this year would be different*, he thought.

"Good morning, rabbits," said Mrs. Carrotson, as she greeted them.

13

"Welcome back to school. To start off, why don't we all join hands in a circle? We'll say our names and tell what our favorite food is."

The rabbits joined hands in a circle. Maria Rabbit went first. "My name is Maria, and I love macaroni."

Just then, Ricky noticed some puzzles at the back of the room. There was one he really wanted to do! It was a picture of outer space.

Ricky ran out of the circle, grabbed the puzzle, and sat down to put it together.

"Ricky Rabbit, come back here," said Mrs. Carrotson.

Ricky shouted back, "I do not feel like doing the circle anymore. Can I put this puzzle together, Mrs. Carrotson? Please?"

"No," said Mrs. Carrotson, "Most certainly not."

Later, when all the rabbits were sitting on the reading rug, Mrs. Carrotson showed them the front cover of a book. She asked, "Who can look at the picture and tell me what the story will be about?"

Ricky shouted out, "It's about…"

"I didn't call on you, Ricky," said Mrs. Carrotson. "If you want to answer a question, please raise your hand."

Maria Rabbit whispered to Rachel Rabbit, "He is SO annoying."

During recess, when all the rabbits were playing hopscotch, it was Ricky's turn. Ricky looked at the court.

"Don't you know how to play?" said Maria. "It's HOPscotch. All rabbits play hopscotch, silly."

"Go ahead, Ricky," the rest of the rabbits teased. "Go ahead and play."

Ricky dropped a rock into the first square. But instead of hopping nicely into the next square, he just zoomed right across the whole hopscotch court.

21

"What's wrong with you?" said Vincent Rabbit.

"You are supposed to hop into the second square, and then the third, fourth and fifth, sixth, seventh, and eighth. Then you hop all the way back and pick up the rock. Watch," said Maria, as she showed off how well she could hop.

The rabbits were all laughing at Ricky. "It's hopscotch. You have to hop."

"I cannot hop," said Ricky, unhappily. "I lost my hop when I was a baby." Ricky could not stand the laughing any longer and off he ran.

Mrs. Carrotson called after him.

"Ricky, come here," she said. "Sit down, please."

Ricky sat down next to her on a large bench.

"You don't understand," he said. "Nobody does."

"I think I do," said Mrs. Carrotson. "When I was little, I didn't have a hop, either."

"You didn't?" said Ricky. He was totally surprised.

"No, I was always racing and running all around," said Mrs. Carrotson.

"Like me?" asked Ricky.

"Yes, a lot like you," answered Mrs. Carrotson.

Mrs. Carrotson gave him a great, big smile. "Sometimes, I drove my teachers crazy."

Then Mrs. Carrotson told Ricky some stories about when she was young, which put a big smile on his face. For the first time, Ricky felt like someone understood him.

The next day, Mrs. Carrotson invited Ricky to come to a meeting, along with his mom and dad.

"When he was a baby, Ricky could hop," said his mom. "But ever since he was a young bunny, he couldn't hop nicely like all the other bunnies. He just ran. We never knew what to do about it."

His dad said, "We took Ricky for a checkup, but Dr. Fluff said there was nothing physically wrong with him."

Mrs. Carrotson said, "Maybe the school guidance counselor can help him." She whispered into Ricky's ear, "My guidance counselor was the one who helped me."

Mr. Sam, the guidance counselor, came to the door. He was a tall rabbit with glasses and a moustache. When he came into the room, he looked at Ricky and asked, "Do you like dinosaurs?"

Ricky answered, "They are my absolute favorite."

Mr. Sam asked, "Okay, what did the rabbit say to the three-headed dinosaur?"

"I don't know," said Ricky.

"Hello, hello, hello," smiled Mr. Sam.

Ricky laughed.

Mr. Sam explained how much he wanted to help Ricky. Ricky liked him right away.

Then, Mr. Sam took Ricky back to see his office. It was filled with lots of pictures other rabbits at school had drawn. He had lots of books and games and stickers.

"Cool," said Ricky.

The next day, Mr. Sam came into Ricky's classroom. Mrs. Carrotson said, "Ricky, Mr. Sam is here for you."

The rabbits in his class asked Ricky, "Where are you going?"

"I am going with Mr. Sam to talk and play games. And then I'll get some stickers."

"Wow," said the other rabbits.

Ricky felt kind of lucky.

They went to Mr. Sam's office.

"Sit down, Ricky," said Mr. Sam.

Mr. Sam looked right at Ricky. Speaking very softly, he said, "Ricky, your teacher tells me that sometimes you do things without thinking."

"I can't help myself," said Ricky.

"Yes, you can," said Mr. Sam. "I will teach you how. It's as easy as 1-2-3."

Mr. Sam explained, "You've got to
       STOP,
       RELAX,
       and
       THINK."

Ricky tried his very best to pay attention.

"The first thing you have to do is STOP. When you think you might do something that could get you in trouble, don't do anything else—just stop. Next, you need to RELAX," explained Mr. Sam.

"How do I relax?" asked Ricky.

"I will teach you deep breathing."

"But I am breathing already," said Ricky.

"We all breathe every day but deep breathing is different. It helps us calm down," said Mr. Sam.

41

Ricky kept listening to Mr. Sam.

"Slowly, you take a deep breath in through your nose. In your mind, you count to 4. Then let the breath out through your mouth, while you slowly count to 4 again. Watch me. I will count to 4 in my own mind. If you like, you can count to 4 out loud."

Mr. Sam took a deep breath in through his nose, and Ricky counted, "1-2-3-4." Then Mr. Sam let the breath out through his mouth, while Ricky counted, "1-2-3-4."

"I want to try it now," said Ricky. Ricky took a deep breath in through his nose and counted in his mind, *1-2-3-4*. Then he let it out, *1-2-3-4*.

"Good," said Mr. Sam. "Now, do it again two more times. I'll do it with you."

After Ricky finished, he said, "Wow, I feel calm."

"Me, too," smiled Mr. Sam.

42

Now, Ricky knew how to stop and how to relax. Next, he needed to learn how to think. Mr. Sam explained that there are good choices and bad choices.

"When you are about to do something, Ricky, you must THINK to yourself: Is this a good choice or a bad choice?"

Mr. Sam showed Ricky some cards that had questions on them. "Here, Ricky, tell me if these choices are good or bad."

Mr. Sam read from the cards, "Okay, here goes. Is cutting ahead on line a good or bad choice?"

"Bad choice," Ricky answered.

"Asking someone if you can please have some of their snack?"

"Good choice," said Ricky.

"Calling out in class?" asked Mr. Sam.

"Bad choice," answered Ricky. "But, sometimes it's hard for me to stop myself from doing it."

"Do you ride a bike, Ricky?" Mr. Sam asked.

"Of course," answered Ricky.

"Remember when you first started? It was hard, and you were probably all wobbly."

"And I fell a few times, too. But now it's easy."

"When you practice your Stop, Relax and Think program, it will get easier and easier."

Over the next few weeks, Ricky tried his Stop, Relax and Think program. At first, it was hard. Then it did get easier and easier—just like Mr. Sam said!

Sometimes he made mistakes, but day by day and week by week, Ricky actually started to like school.

During recess, Ricky watched as the other rabbits played hopscotch.

"Go ahead and play, too," said Mrs. Carrotson.

"But you have to hop for hopscotch," said Ricky, feeling a little worried.

"Please come and play," said Maria.

53

Ricky looked at the boxes. He dropped a rock into the first square and hopped into box 2. Then he hopped into box 3 and 4 and 5 and 6 and 7 and 8. The rabbits cheered. Ricky turned around, hopped all the way back, and picked up the rock.

All the rabbits shouted, "Ricky hopped! Hop, hop, hooray!"

"What a wonderful day," smiled Mrs. Carrotson, and she snapped a photo, which still hangs in Mr. Sam's office.

"We're all so proud of you," said Mrs. Carrotson.

"I'm proud of me, too," said Ricky. "And I think that's the best proud there is!"